Snow W

D0371887

By Melissa Lagonegro

Illustrated by Artful Doodlers

Random House New York

Copyright © 2005 Disney Enterprises, Inc. All rights reserved under International and Pan-American Copyright Conventions. Published in the United States by Random House Children's Books, a division of Random House, Inc., New York, NY 10019, and simultaneously in Canada by Random House of Canada Limited, Toronto, in conjunction with Disney Enterprises, Inc. RANDOM HOUSE and colophon are registered trademarks of Random House, Inc.

Library of Congress Control Number: 2004093748 ISBN: 0-7364-2326-5

www.randomhouse.com/kids/disney

MANUFACTURED IN CHINA

10 9 8 7 6 5 4 3 2 1

I have a secret, but you must promise not to tell anyone. Since I've been married to the Prince, I don't get to visit the Dwarfs very often. We always had such fun together, and they enjoyed having my help around the cottage.

But here's my secret—I still help the Dwarfs. They just don't know it.

Every once in a while, I sneak off to the Dwarfs' little cottage in the woods. I hide and wait for them to leave for the mines. It's such fun knowing that the Dwarfs will have a clean and cozy cottage to come home to when I'm finished.

As soon as the Dwarfs are out of sight,
my little bluebird friend sings a sweet tune.
Then I sneak into the cottage and get started.

I wouldn't get anything done without my animal friends. They help me tidy up, and they're very good at keeping a secret.

There's a lot of work to do if I want the cottage to look its best! But first I open all the windows. The cool forest breeze always makes the cottage smell fresh and clean.

Then we get right to work! I sweep the floors while the squirrels dust the shelves and the birds remove the cobwebs. The chipmunks and the deer wash and dry the dishes.

After finishing downstairs, we head upstairs to tidy the bedroom. I make the Dwarfs' seven little beds and fluff all the pillows. I even fold Grumpy's blanket just the way he likes it. I know that brings a smile to his face.

SNEEZY

When the cottage is clean from top to bottom, I add the finishing touches—that's always my favorite part. I go into the woods and search for the most beautiful flowers. Sometimes I pick daisies, and other times I pick lilies. Flowers always make the cottage look and smell wonderful.

But the Dwarfs' special surprise wouldn't be complete without some tasty snacks. I gather lots of fruits, nuts, and berries in the forest and leave them for the Dwarfs to enjoy. They especially love gooseberries. Dopey can eat a whole basketful by himself!

When the little bluebird sings his sweet song, I must quickly finish my work—the Dwarfs are on their way home, and I don't want to be seen.

I hide beside the cottage and wait for them to enter. I love watching their reactions when they see their special surprise.

I try very hard to keep my visits a secret. But once, I took off my necklace so it wouldn't get dirty—and I left it on the kitchen table! Luckily, a squirrel snatched it back for me before the Dwarfs got home.

Another time, when the Dwarfs returned home, Happy had an especially big smile on his face. Doc thought Happy had sneaked away from the mines during lunch to clean up the cottage.

Dopey thought Sneezy had done all the cleaning and dusting, because he was extra sneezy.

Bashful just knew it had to be Sleepy, because he was especially tired.

Each Dwarf thought another Dwarf had made the cottage so lovely. No one suspected me!

For a while, the Dwarfs thought that the forest animals fixed up their cottage. If they only knew that the animals had a lot of help—from me, of course! But I'll never tell the Dwarfs, because it's such fun keeping it a secret.

Now, my secret is just between you, my animal friends, and me. Don't tell anyone—especially the Dwarfs!